# HIDDEN WORDS

An anthology of works by the thinkarts Creative Writing Group

# About "Hidden Words" and the thinkarts Creative Writing Group

The thinkarts Creative Writing Group has been meeting in Ilford since July 2009, as a forum for mental health service users in North East London with an interest in writing. It provides a friendly and encouraging environment, where participants are challenged to attempt different forms and topics of writing and hone their skills. Group members appreciate the opportunity to meet as writers, share their work and inspire each other to greater literary achievements. Originally facilitated by a thinkarts link worker and occupational therapist, the group has now become self-sustained and participant-led and continues to build on a supportive foundation.

***"I come to the group for the company of fellow writers. There is a genuine camaraderie and I learn a lot about creative writing skills."*** Azeem Khan

This anthology is the first publication of the group's work. Individual authors have also had work published. The content of this anthology has been collected over many writing sessions, each with its own topic. Whilst this work encompasses the various aspects of human life, it brings a particular focus to issues that often marginalise individuals in society. These include mental illness, loneliness, fear, bullying, loss, stress and politics. But throughout these pages runs a strand of hope, carefully woven amongst nostalgic and satirical compositions.

We hope you are inspired by this collection to capture your journey on paper.

**Please note:**
**The content of this book is for adult readership only. The text contains crude language or depictions in parts.**

**The works, names and places in this collection are fictional and expressions of the creative imaginings of the authors. Where reference is made to real characters or places, this is done in the interest of fictional writing. Content should not be seen as fact or taken as medical advice.**

# Contents

## Poetic Advice

A nervous laugh comes to the lips,
On being asked for poetical tips,
You never need to rhyme he quips,
For you could have an ending like
Toodle pips.

**By Robin Dixon**

We hear

## Music

I am the music a harp and a flute,
to the melody I gently salute.
I am a romping child happily dancing,
I am a little lady happily prancing.

Beautiful notes all of a whirl,
the music of life all of a twirl.
The colours of sound is all that we need,
dance with me and I will take the lead.

I am a song bird singing so bright,
with me the music sounds so right.
Tuneful and joyful a harmony just,
music forever - simply a must.

**by Beverley Harknett**

## The Disco Era

The disco era has just begun
Everybody's having fun
As far as you can see
The crowd, as happy as can be

The pub venues were of plenty
For under 18's and over twenty
DJ plays the sounds of today
Everybody dance! The night away

The year, Seventy Seven
A dance sound, 'Seventh Heaven'
Is playing on the radio
A mid tempo song that's on the go

Now everybody get up and groove
And make your body move
Dancing to the disco beat
While you dance upon your happy feet

And so, that's the way it used to be
When we were young, single and free
The disco era, we once knew
While we dance the whole night through.

**By Michael Feldman**

## Music makes my world go round

Music makes my world go round
As I imagine myself moving round and around
It uplifts my mood
As it should

I take myself to the dance floor
As I am unsure
That across the world
Music is wild

I see red, pink and purple
And I eat the apple
All the lyrics
Are painted in acrylics.

**By S.S.**

## Playing the piano after 40 years

Wrong notes, hesitant fingers
Begin again, as memory lingers
Key stretches, to reach base line
Shock memory of forgotten time.

**By Anon**

## Music Scene

Picture a scene
of all in between
like a dream
I mean

Could be about
life or love
or some of
the above

Visions
Decisions

Variety
A sight to see

Destiny or fate
memories or images
lets create.

**By Robert Philcox**

## A poem about classical music

The passion of a Beethoven composition
Is as great as Mozart in transition
The romance of Tchaikovsky's Swan Lake
Is sufficient to keep one awake

And Rimsky Korsakov's Scheherazade
To listen to is not very hard
And Mendelssohn's A Midsummer Night's Dream
Is fantasy almost to the extreme.

**By David Berlevy**

We feel

## In my arms

In my arms I carry you little one
For that's where you belong,
You are lovely and cuddly to hold to me
And you respond with a coo and ba-ba

I sing a song la-la-la and it soothes you
Until you go to sleep
And while you are dreaming, I prepare your meal
And what's on your menu today? I wonder

You wake with a cry
And in response to your needs
I cuddle you and give you the warm milk
Which I prepared especially for you,
And it's time for more cuddles and play, for
You do belong in my arms.

**By S.S.**

## A Fish and Chips Dinner

I invited my friend
Round to dine
I see her from
Time to time
I said I'd like to cook
So she gave me a knowing look

Fish and chips for tea
Just for you and me
Do you like the cutlery?
Would you like a drink?
Yes I would she said,

Red wine would be fine

Would you like some music?
Some rhythm and rhyme
After our dinner
Our arms entwine

A friendly cuddle and a hug
As we sit beside the fireside
On my new rug

Then after everything had ended
She said thanks its all been splendid.

**By Robert Philcox**

## 'A-pizza-the-action'

A satirical poem about a meal, with an Elizabethan feel to it

'Twas on New Year's eve night,
That I invited William Shakespeare to a meal,
With six Tudor chairs and candlelight,
A Christmas tree in a corner such delight,
Then a tuna and anchovy pizza was laid,
Upon the table, Queen Elizabeth displayed,
The virgin queen then produced soft drinks,
Shakespeare expected alcohol methinks,
The Italian cheese and tomato smelt divine,
And then Queen Elizabeth brought in the wine
"At last" proclaimed Shakespeare with great pleasure,
For Queen Elizabeth is our national treasure.

**By David Berlevy**

## Come For Dinner

I asked my friend, I've known some time
to be my guest and come for dinner
I'm cooking fish with a little thyme
His favourite dish, sure is a winner

The table is arranged with cutlery
His choice of beer or juice desired
Like orange, apple, cranberry
Is sure likely to be admired

So I arrange the room, dim the lights
He's coming here soon, I know
Travelling through the misty night
Not to mention wind, rain and snow

With so much time spent tidying up
Waiting for my friend to arrive
I'm drinking from my favourite cup
Relaxing before the stroke of five

At 5pm I welcome then, with a friendly smile
What a dreadful night I happen to say
The weather will be like this for a while
I add, while welcoming him to stay.

**By Michael Feldman**

## The Kittens

Two months ago a cat with kittens appeared
at the back of our house, tiny cats had been reared,
a gold tortoiseshell cat with four young
possibly abandoned as no ID tags round the necks were hung,
not knowing whether they were feral or tame,
lost to the world and without name,
hungry and thirsty I fed them with cat meat,
the mother cat ate heartily as kittens surrounded her feet,
for a week they were fed and stayed together,
then they disappeared as unpredictable as the weather.

**By David Berlevy**

## The Etiquette of Messaging

Yunus was curled up in the foetal position, fast asleep in bed, when his mobile phone rang at 3:37 a.m. with the irritating insistent bleeping that meant he had received a text. Startled and groggy, he looked at the phone, and was suddenly angry that it showed Darren's name on the phone as the sender. The text read:

I'm outside. Where are you?

It was a cryptic, imponderable, yet stupid message. If Darren was outside, where exactly was he at that time of night? Outside where? Yunus fell back into bed, cursing his friend, and bitter for having been woken up. It took him ages to get back to sleep again.
For the next few days, he was still angry with Darren for his prank. When Darren rang him on Saturday, asking Yunus if he wanted to come around for a drink, Yunus snapped.
'Why the hell d'you ring me in the middle of the night?'
'It was only a joke!' cried Darren.
'Well I'm done with your stupid jokes. It took me bloody ages to get to sleep again that night.'
There was a pregnant pause.
'I've had just about enough out of you,' hissed Yunus.
'You're taking it too seriously,' Darren said.
'You're damn right I am. You're going manic again, that's what it is'.
'Rubbish!'
'Yes you are. You're awake at all hours, pissing people off. You'll end up back in hospital, I know it.'
'So you're a doctor now are you, Yunus?'
'Get lost, Darren. Don't ring me again, in the middle of the night. On second thought, don't ring me at all.'
Yunus put down the phone, relieved to be rid of the pest who called himself a friend. Although he was glad he had told Darren not to bother him again, a part of Yunus felt guilty too. He remembered walking the corridors of Lilac Ward, himself diagnosed with manic depression, and feeling lonely and bitter. The boredom was the worst part of being incarcerated in a psychi-

atric hospital. Darren had come up to him, and offered him his friendship without condition, rather like a lovesick puppy dog. Yunus, who was going through a lot of personal trauma, welcomed Darren's beguiling, stupid smile and his crude jokes. It helped in Lilac Ward to have somebody on your side, to wile away the tedium and to smoke endless cigarettes with.
Over the coming months, once they were both discharged from hospital, Yunus and Darren saw more and more of one another, becoming regulars at the local cinema, where they devoured mountains of popcorn and consumed the mindless Hollywood drivel of the multiplex. They would eat together at the variety of Pakistani restaurants in Ilford Lane, getting fat on the oily food and enjoying their basic level of brotherhood.

That was three years ago. Since then, Darren got divorced from his wife and broke up with his own family, becoming a bitter, angry recluse. He shunned Yunus for a long time and the two became strangers. Then, by chance, the pair met on the busy Ilford Lane one spring day, and exchanged numbers. Both men had moved addresses since their last meeting. Yunus was disappointed that Darren was now an embittered cynic, angry at the way the world had treated him. But he was content to meet his old friend for a cosy cup of tea every week.
Yunus would turn up at Darren's flat on a Tuesday afternoon, and endure Darren's tirade of abuse against the politicians of the day, or of the idiocies of TV celebrities or the shortcomings of the council...the victims of his anger were many and varied, and gradually Yunus, who occasionally spoke his mind, grew fed up with the abuse. It was hard to get a word in when Darren was in full flow. When Yunus did offer an opinion, it was quickly criticised by Darren. Yunus was made to feel naïve and grew irritated eventually with simply being a passive listener to Darren's rants.
Eventually Yunus stopped coming around on Tuesdays to Darren's. When Darren asked him what the reason was for his not coming, Yunus got annoyed with having to lie about being too busy elsewhere. It had been 3 weeks since his last visit to Darren's that the text message came at 3:37 a.m.

I'm outside. Where are you?

A week later, sitting in his armchair at home, smoking a cigarette, Yunus felt

lonely once again. He had nobody to turn to. The TV had a mindless day-time chat show on and he was bored. Yunus had no job to go to and he was single – girls were not exactly banging on the door to be let in. It was also a Tuesday.
Yunus picked up his phone and thought about Darren. He would be at home at this time too, doing nothing, unemployed as well.
Putting out his cigarette, Yunus dialled.
'Hi Darren. It's me. Can I come around?'

**By Azeem Khan**

## Up and Down

You feel all alone.
No one is there to help you,
No one there to talk with you,
No one to have a laugh with you.

The phone rings.
A friend is on the line,

You smile, you talk you laugh,
Arrangements are made to meet,
You go out and have a good time.

Then you get back,
And no one is there...,
You feel all alone.

**By Robin Dixon**

## I miss you

Time will pass, if I let it,
It will pass me by,
like the people in the crowds.

I miss you.

They say time heals,
sometimes it does,
often it doesn't,
Your presence taken from me,
so sudden and so quick.

I miss you.

I loved your face,
your happy face,
your warm voice and
comforting smile –
Death is deep, bereavement deeper.

I miss you.

Still.

**By Beverley Harknett**

We imagine

## From a carving

Upright, her feet embedded, very still
You could put her on your window sill
Arms hanging limply by her sides
Feelings she attempts to hide

Head and arms are what you see
The rest of her is left to be
Stone that blends into a base
Calm expression on her face

She is an animal carved in stone
Standing here all on her own
Each straight hair detailed with care
Viewers you just stand and stare

**By Anon**

# Soapy

I wonder why he doesn't come in any more. He used to take such pride in his appearance. Every morning he would come in and wash his face (and nearly bald head). Then he'd have a shave and brush what remained of his teeth. In the evening he would take a bath. To think he used to talk to me whenever he lathered me up. "Soap for Soapy" he used to cackle. Silly old sod. He must stink to hell now.

All I have for company at the moment are flies - far too many of them, and spiders - not enough of them! The only noises I hear are the postman delivering the odd letter and the occasional knocking at the front door. There was someone doing that this morning. The racket that was made! I didn't think the place would remain standing with that ferocity of the knocking. Whoever it was couldn't rouse him and went away, eventually. Just like all the others. Why is he so quiet? He must be very stealthy because I never hear him move around. I don't even hear him put on the television or radio nowadays. What...

The door knocker always makes me jump. Now they're at the letterbox. Nosey sods! What's that!?! If they keep that up then the entire building is going to fall down...

"You need to go to the gym for some workouts Jones. You should have had that door down with one kick."

"I didn't hear you offering to show me how it's done Sarge. Goodness! What a stink!"

"Cover your mouth and nose with your hankie, like this. Now follow me in... Here he is. He probably pegged out while he was watching the telly".

"I'm going to throw up Sar..."

"Not here you don't".

"But...but..."

"But nothing! Until they tell us otherwise this is a crime scene. Get out! Now!"

"Urrrrrrgh..."

"Poor old bugger. I've never seen so many flies. I'm surprised there's anything left of him. He must have been dead for ages, and to think the only person who cared to contact us was a bloke from the gas board. And that was only because wanted access so he could cut him off. Oh well, I suppose I'd better see how Jones is before contacting the station."

So that's what happened. But why am I feeling so strange? There are drops of water coming down my side, yet there isn't anywhere for them to come from. Now they're coming faster and faster. I am lathering up, but Soapy isn't here. The water keeps coming. I don't understand...

**By Robin Dixon**

## Mr Robin's achievement

He sat quietly; holding his chin above his head as he boldly planned his daily work and the achievements he had already made. Having second thoughts this time, Mr Robin retrieved a large envelope from one of the chests of drawers located in his little old study room. He pulled out and read the contents that were inside, it seemed as though it was some kind of business letter because it had a bearing of the company.

After reading the letter three or four times, Mr Robin showed a smile of gratitude and excitement. Leaning forward he put his reading glasses on and grabbed a black pen that has his name imprinted on it, then he gazed at the window for a minute and this time he started writing a letter replying to the one read.

Mr Robin was very talented artist who would usually put his skills into use. In his letter Mr Robin was invited to attend and take part in a Christmas play in one of the ART Performing Studios located in Waltham Forest. So Mr Robin did not waste time - he quickly accepted the invitation.

When he had finished replying to the letter, Mr Robin pulled out a large brown envelope from another set of drawers. After putting his letter inside, he sealed the envelope and neatly addressed it to the manager "MR JONES", and then he put a stamp on it and put it on the desk ready for posting. He then made himself a quick cup of tea and retired to bed till next morning.

**By S.S.**

## The Eighties

Margaret Thatcher was Tory's guide,
There was a lot of pride,
Yet, there were many demonstrations,
By miners, anti-poll-tax and other organisations,
People went on riots and went berserk,
In tennis Navratilova took over from Billie Jean King,
Michael Jackson and Madonna made everybody sing,
But John Lennon was killed in New York City,
Which ended a Beatles reunion, what a pity.
The world watched the Live Aid concert on T.V.
To raise money for the Ethiopian Famine plea,
Wars across the Middle East were raging,
Whilst the communist block was disengaging.

**By David Berlevy**

## Thomas Wolfe

It was the time of rage
Where the fight was lifted from the page

Sometimes it felt like being in a cage
This was real life not actors on the stage

The war was rough but never smooth
It almost felt like being a stooge

We were pawns for our government
We weren't always well spent

We are fighting for our cause
We don't expect applause

It's our freedom we respect
And our world we protect

War is a bad idea
We should try to get along in peace
And sort out the problems more sincere.

Just before the war ended Thomas Wolfe
Thought he saw a glimpse into the
future

Where some people pretend
We sometimes put our trust in a friend

We no longer have rations
Such things are out of fashion

Life can be a passion
Love is compassion

Life is very fast today
Before you look it's gone away

Into another day
Before we grasp I would like to say

Enjoy all the pleasures of the future
Including phones and home computers

This future can sometimes seem bizarre
People driving faster cars.

**By Robert Philcox**

We write

## A first attempt at Haiku

The writer's group
is good for practice
on lined pages.

**By Michael Feldman**

## Voice

Walking
Inside I am talking
I baulk
Yet stalking
Thoughts
Catching oughts
And shoulds
Using coulds
And woulds
Sorting
Choices

**By Anon**

## A city gent

One day, I was on a train when I began to eavesdrop on someone trying to have a conversation with a worker from the city, a real city gent. He certainly looked the part with his black suite, waist coat and bowler hat; ready to start the working day. The fellow, whom I didn't know from 'Adam' as the saying goes, started to ask the gentleman unusual questions that even I would not have the nerve to ask. In front of other passengers the fellow said: 'Excuse me, but don't you think it rather old fashioned of you to be dressed in the clothes that you are wearing?' adding. 'After all, you don't see anyone else dressed like you are. If it was the 1940's, then that would have been a different story.'

The gentleman politely gave the fellow a chance to speak, but then retorted. 'How dare you insult me by the way I dress? It is none of your business!' With this, the fellow was taken aback and remained speechless.

While all of this was going on, I was listening to what the gentleman and the fellow were saying. After a few 'choice' words I decided to intervene on the fellow's behalf because by then, it appeared that the situation was getting a bit heated, yet none of the other passengers had decided to become involved.

So, there I was, alone and not knowing exactly what to say. I approached the gentleman, telling him that the fellow did not mean any offense. I offered to him that I have autism and wondered if the fellow may have similar difficulties, as I had observed his behaviour to be as such. At this point, the gentleman said that he did not know what autism was. I explained to him that my understanding of autism is that it is a disability affecting social and communication skills but not necessarily intelligence. I went on to say, that I too have 'slipped up' in the past. The gentleman then said: 'That's no excuse for his behaviour.' Eventually, I managed to calm the situation by saying that he was sorry and that somehow I too managed to use social skills learnt by attending a few courses.

By the time I calmed the situation, the train arrived at the gentleman's stop in the city, by which time he was in a better frame of mind because of my efforts.

**By Michael Feldman**

## Why me?

Why me why you
Is this wrong
Is this right
This feeling I fight
Is it instinctive
Is this true
Days come to pass
It doesn't make a difference
Which class
We belong as much as any other
I carry on and so should you
Be confident be strong
Whistle your favourite song
While you work along
The future is today
Memories of good will stay
Personally I am feeling well
Most of the time
Have a drink, pour some wine
Or tee total - that's also fine
Sometimes the pictures in my head don't connect
With what you said
But mostly now I feel fine
The demons are gone
Now that's fine hopefully
They won't return for a while
I'll take this time to enjoy
And try to forget any sadness
Fill my heart with thoughts
Of gladness.

**By Robert Philcox**

## An Electric Light Bulb Saved My Life

Most of my friendships have been formed
Under the light of a bulb;
Areas of light and dark, separating good from evil;
I had an electric shock as a young boy
When I stuck my finger in the light bulb socket.

Recovery followed pain, and the light bulb
Framed many surprises
Between brainwaves and bold moments.

I recall a nightmare, my sweaty body and the terror of the dark;
Snap on the electric light and the bulb illuminates a hundred ideas.

Many gruesome discoveries are made with the help of a light bulb;
Professional police images crafted with a photographer's light bulb.

Light speed bathes me
186,000 miles per second
Yet it's easily smashed
Fragile is a light bulb.

**By Azeem Khan**

## The Colours

I see your face shine yellow in the sun
You said your life has just begun

I say you are like a myriad of colours
You could be like flowers
I could talk to you for hours

Your favourite colour is blue
I said yes that is true
You like to wear trainers
I like to wear shoes

You don't smoke or drink much booze
I want your company soon
Like walking in the afternoon

I like the colours of a rainbow
You keep your thoughts in tow.

**By Robert Philcox**

## Envelop Your Feelings

You articulate your feelings,
About the relationship,
In a letter to your beloved.

Looking for an envelope,
You can only find one,
With a window.

So you write the address,
On the back of the letter,
Placing it in the envelope,
Concealing the zigzag green,
Ensuring the address can be seen,
You seal it with a loving kiss

And mail it first class,
Hoping for the reply,
That does not say,
Return to sender.

**By Robin Dixon**

We aspire

Waiting
And waiting
All day long for the call
That so far hasn't come
Waiting fifteen years
For the chance that never comes
One morning it will rain
Water falling from Heaven on my face
Washing away my sins
The journey to Hollywood
Starts with a single step
I don't need the call
I'm closer to the setting sun
Than yesterday.

**By Azeem Khan**

# Aiming to Publish My Life Story

While at boarding school and in my early teens, I kept a diary of day-to-day events. It was, I suppose, one way of expressing my true feelings in certain situations. Back then, I was having episodes of emotional turmoil - this being the norm for most teenagers, although all the more for me because of my autism. Autism is a disability affecting communication skills and not necessarily intelligence. Although, having said this, I do have a form of a specific learning difference or learning difficulty in simpler 'layman's terms'.

After leaving school, I continued to keep a diary. From here, I progressed to writing correspondence to various publications such as Record Mirror and then, the local periodical, the Hackney Gazette where, over the years, I remained successful in having my letters published.

The idea of writing a book came in 2000. My mother at the time and to get me started, narrated the events surrounding my life. I then added the various events taking place until leaving school back in 1967.

My aim, eventually, is to get my book published. First, I need to gain enough writing skills so that everything flows without 'struggling' to find the right words. Writing is a skill that needs to be learnt, and for some it doesn't come easy. It is not unusual for the writer to frequently amend the contents, before presenting to the publishers a product appealing to a wide audience.

Before moving to Ilford in 2003, I attended a writers' surgery where I saw a professional author. She told me that the manuscript contents failed to appeal to an audience. However, after a certain amount of time lapsed, I did appraise the chapters in my write ups pertaining to my first 16 years of life. Yet, something continued to appear missing. I was lacking details and needed to amend everything written to this point.

While I am still learning about how to write my life story, it remains helpful to continue attending my fortnightly writers' group to improve my skills. I can also attend another writer's surgery or try, somehow, to learn to put my life story together. Then, I should be in business once I can 'capture an audience' and gain some recognition from the relevant publishers themselves.

**By Michael Feldman**

## A Poem about Stress and Staying Mentally Well in Hard Times

In order to stay mentally well,
it is not easy in the modern day,
it means having to avoid doing certain things,
or being able to not get too bothered,
it is difficult to stay unaffected
when a recession has burdened us all
it has caused pubs to close,
gym classes to be cancelled,
people to lose their jobs,
friendships to fracture and fail,
people to feel dejected and miserable,
which makes it harder to feel well,
also people less want to go out,
even watching television would be stressful,
a televised football match could be hell,
or listening to it on a radio commentary
attempting to listening to music on the radio,
interrupted by annoying advertisements,
sitting in the sunshine when is not raining,
looking on the internet for things to do,
hoping that it does not crash or slow down,
texting people on mobiles, who are busy,
avoid travelling when buses or tubes are crowded,
which means not in rush hour or when children come home,
it's impossible with road works all over,
but cycling in the road is dangerous,
even walking in the street is a risk
you never know when a mugger will approach you,
as London is very stressful to live in,
there are knifings, shootings and ASBOS,
Saturday nights are not much fun now,
bouncers search you for weapons on entry,
people look at you as if you are abnormal
especially if you are on your own

people with mental health problems,
are stigmatised wherever they go,
employers don't want them to work for them,
nobody understands the way they are,
which makes them more isolated,
more likely to avoid people and places,
which leaves them staying alone at home.
Thus the answer to staying mentally well,
is to focus on relaxation, yoga and meditation
which can be done in a safe calm place,
away from prying eyes and criticism,
where no one can cause you harm
and where you can have peace and quiet.

**By David Berlevy**

## Eyes Of The Soul

It is with great trust that we look into
the eyes of another person,
as the soul maybe mirrored
behind their vision.
And it maybe weeping.
we cannot be sure.

But it could be laughing,
giggling in the sun, the rain,
dreaming about moonlit clouds
wafting over dark night skies.
We just do not know.

However, we can trust,
that behind a person's eyes,
will be the experience of life.
They must allow you the viewer
the privilege to see,
everything that hurts, and everything
that doesn't.

So look deep, look sincerely,
Into the windows of their life,
they have trusted you to simply
trust them.
And it is so much to ask for
if we are truly honest,
because as we delve into someone's
beautiful soul,
we come to realise –
It's probably the only one they will ever have.
Who knows.

**By Beverley Harknett**

## The world won't miss you for a while

Disappear, vanish, vamoose,
The world won't miss you for a while,
Have a break, turn your phone off,
The world won't miss you for a while,
Read those books that have been piling up,
The world won't miss you for a while,
Put your feet up, listen to some music,
The world won't miss you for a while,
Relax, don't worry, have a break,
We can get by without you -
But only for a while!

**By Robin Dixon**

water lily house
water lily flowers
Electric Blue, Stowaway
bright yellow centres

**By Anon**

## About the authors:

**David Berlevy**
has always wanted to be a writer because of a vivid literary imagination. His interests are writing, karaoke and playing Scrabble.

**Robin Dixon**
is from Barking. He is involved in a wide range of art activities, including participating in ARC Community Theatre.

**Michael Feldman**
likes writing because it helps him to express himself more effectively. He is currently documenting his autobiography. His hobbies are photography, surfing the internet and writing.

**Beverley Harknett**
has enjoyed writing since her teenage years and finds it to be extremely therapeutic. She has had fifteen poems published and has worked for Waltham Forest Guardian as a theatre and exhibition reviewer. She likes to write every day and finds it gives her great joy and satisfaction.

**Azeem Khan**
is an award-winning film director and author, born in Pakistan in 1965. He is married and lives in Redbridge.

**Anon**
has found new ways of writing being in this creative group.

**Robert Philcox**
used to read and write short stories and songs in his younger years. When he was in hospital, he would write poems to keep occupied. He still has a strong poetic talent and interests in music and science fiction.

**S.S.**
is talented and creative. She likes to take new skills and knowledge on board and enjoys using her hands in a very constructive way.

## Index of work by author: